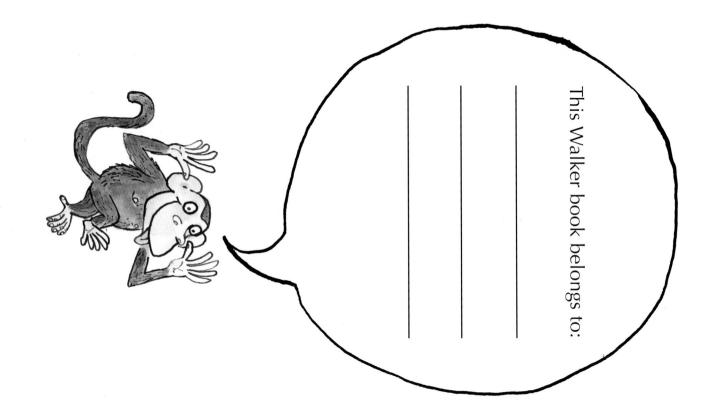

This Walker book belongs to:

First published 1987 by Walker Books Ltd
87 Vauxhall Walk, London SE11 5HJ

This edition published 2015

2 4 6 8 10 9 7 5 3 1

© 1987 Colin West

The right of Colin West to be identified as author/illustrator of this work
has been asserted by him in accordance with the Copyright, Designs and Patents Act 1988

This book has been typeset in Optima

Printed in China

British Library Cataloguing in Publication Data:
a catalogue record for this book is available from the British Library

ISBN 978-1-4063-6751-5

www.walker.co.uk

"Not Me," Said the Monkey

Colin West

WALKER BOOKS
AND SUBSIDIARIES
LONDON · BOSTON · SYDNEY · AUCKLAND

"Who keeps dropping banana skins round here?" growled the lion.

"Not me," said the monkey.

"Who keeps walking all over me?" hissed the snake.

"Not me," growled the lion.
"And not me," said the monkey.

"Who keeps throwing coconuts about?" snorted the rhino.

"Not me," hissed the snake.
"Not me," growled the lion.
"And not me," said the monkey.

"WHO KEEPS TICKLING ME?"
roared the elephant.

"Not me," snorted the rhino.
"Not me," hissed the snake.
"Not me," growled the lion.

Slurp! Slurp! Slurp! went the elephant.

"And not ME!" said the monkey.

WHOOOOOSH!

"Now who's going to stop all this monkey business?" laughed the lion, and the snake, and the rhino, and the elephant

"Well..."

"NOT ME!" said You-Know-Who.

Colin West says everyone loves monkeys and chimps, "probably because they remind us of ourselves so much!"

In "*Not me,*" *said the Monkey* he was keen to create a cheeky character that actually had the last laugh.

Colin says, "Maybe you've been called a 'cheeky monkey' before – but I hope not too often! By the way, did you notice that the front endpapers are different to those at the end?"